For Paxton

A FEIWEL AND FRIENDS BOOK
An Imprint of Holtzbrinck Publishers

Library of Congress Cataloging-in-Publication Data
Wright, Michael
Jake stays awake / written and illustrated by Michael Wright. — 1st ed.
p. cm.   I. Title.   PS3623.R557J35 2007
813'.6 — dc22   2006036339

ISBN-13: 978-0-312-36797-8
ISBN-10: 0-312-36797-x

First Edition: October 2007

10   9   8   7   6   5   4   3   2   1

The text type is set in 32-point Hank.
Book design by Rich Deas

www.feiwelandfriends.com

JAKE

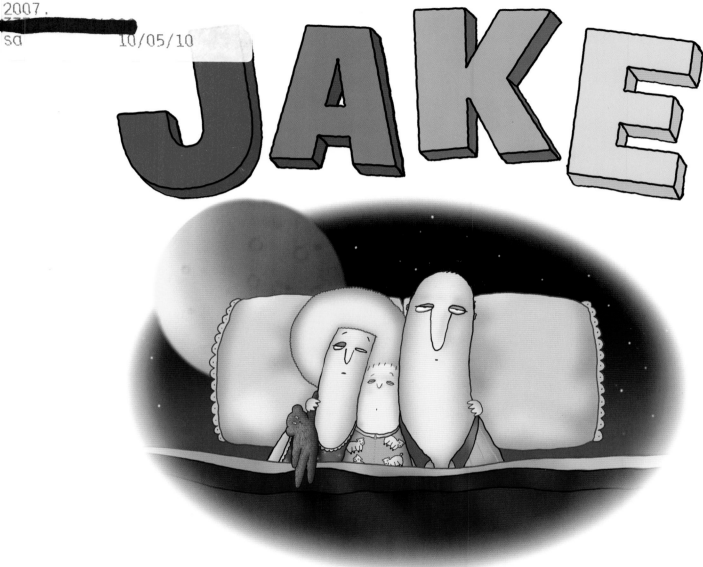

STAYS AWAKE

By Michael Wright

FEIWEL AND FRIENDS
New York

There was a little boy
whose name was Jake
and every night
he'd stay awake.

"Unless I can sleep
with my parents," he said,
"I won't close my eyes,
and I won't go to bed!"

So every night around ten forty-four,
he'd wander on up to his mom and dad's door,
and stand there and knock, till they finally said,
"All right, all right, Jake! You can sleep in our bed."

This drove his poor parents
straight up a tree—they
had a bed made for two,
not a bed made for three.

"We love you, dear Jake,
but we can't even doze.
How can we sleep
with your toes
up our nose?"

SNIFF
SNIFF

But night after night,
for a moment of rest,
they let Jake climb in.
They thought
it was best.

And that's when they knew
something had to be done.
Their sleeping arrangements
were no longer fun.

So his mother and father
thought hard and thought long,
and came up with a plan that
just couldn't go wrong.

Jake considered their offer a second or two,
then, smiling, he said, "I know just what to do!"
He headed outside and pointed straight up.

"Uh-ohh," thought his parents. "No way!"
thought his pup.

Then they climbed to the roof
and attempted to sleep,
but sleep's pretty tricky
on something so steep.

Then nervously Jake said,
"Perhaps we should try
finding some other spot
that's not quite so high."

Jake climbed up the stairs
and said, "Let's all sleep here!"
But that turned out to be
a big pain in the rear.

Jake jumped in the bathtub with his rubber duck,

then in popped his parents and they *all* got stuck.

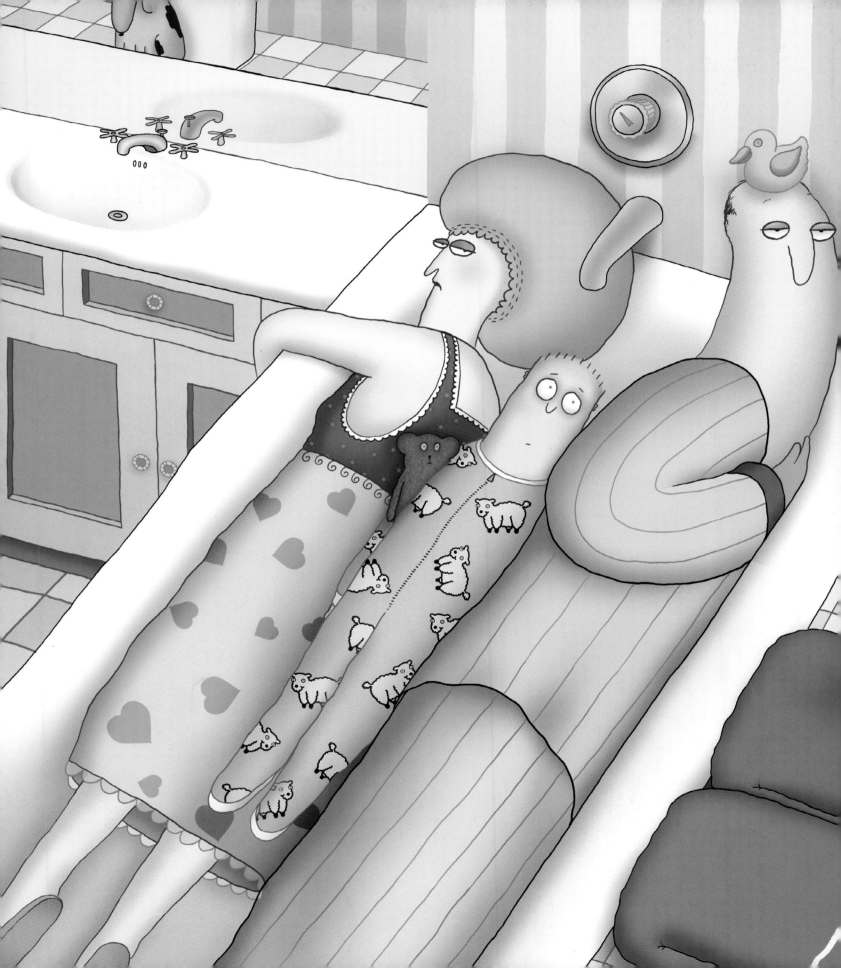

He thought that the kitchen might be a good place,

but it's tough to sleep when you're feeding your face.

The garbage cans seemed
a great idea at first,
till things started stinking
like old liverwurst.

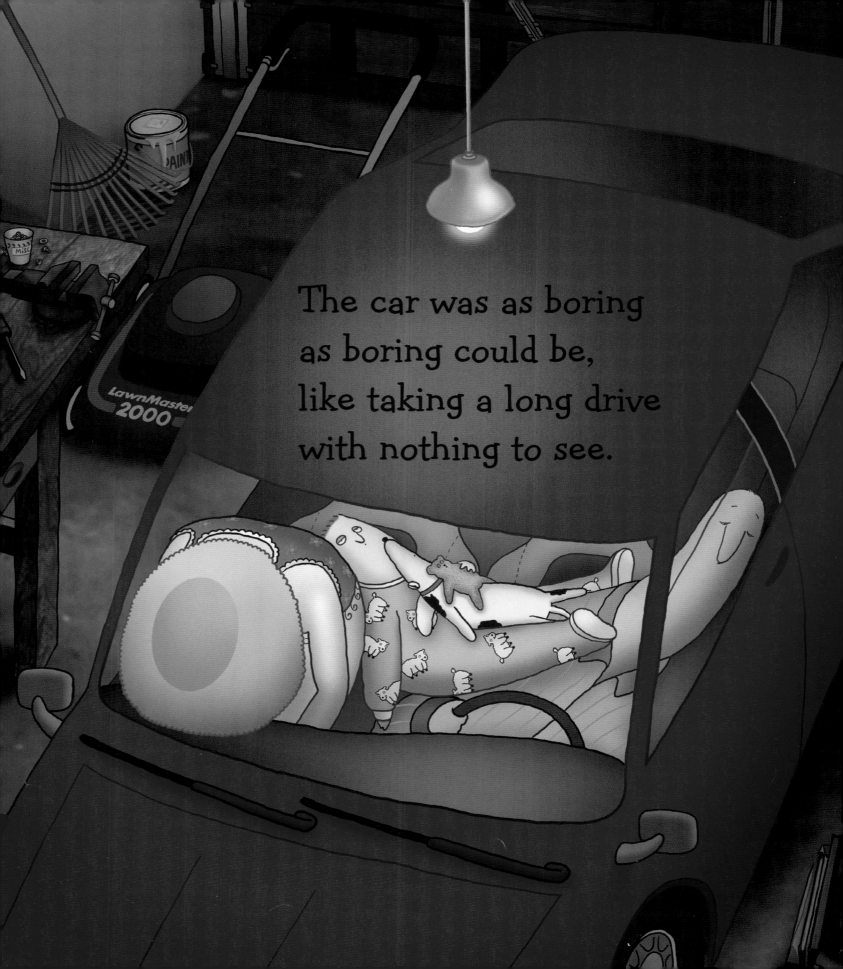

The car was as boring
as boring could be,
like taking a long drive
with nothing to see.

As he lay there and listened to his parents snore,
Jake thought of the one place he hadn't before.

Instead of the roof, or the stairs, or the bath,
instead of the kitchen, the car, or the trash,
Jake thought that his bed didn't sound quite
so bad, so he whispered, "Good night" to his
mom and his dad.

Jake walked himself back to bed in his room, where he slept without moving till quarter to noon.

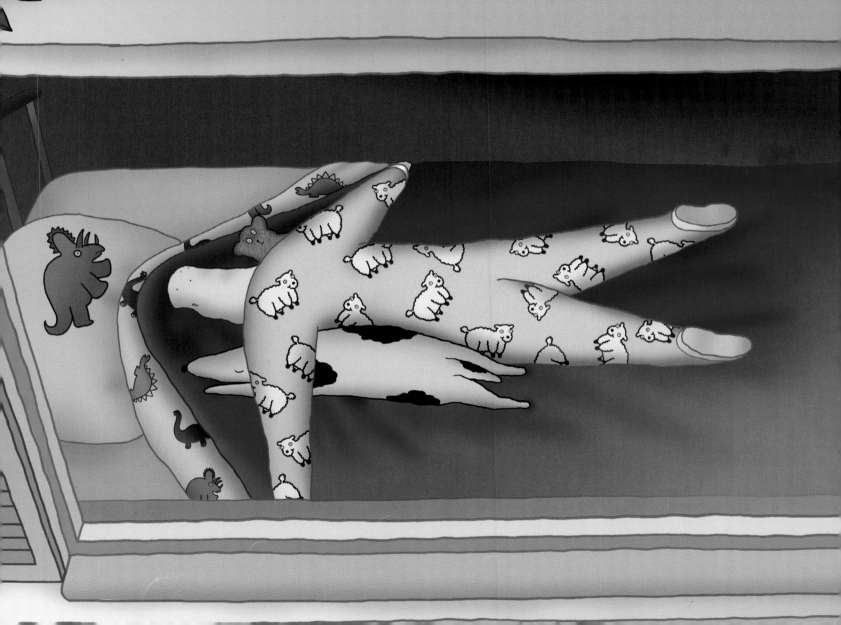

His parents are happy again
with their son,
and everyone's realized
it's not always fun
to have kids sleep with parents
night after night.

But every once in a while?
Well, that's quite all right.